EXTRAORDINARY ORDINARY
Ella

written by
Amber Hendricks

illustrated by
Luciana Navarro Powell

amicus ink

Mankato, Minnesota

To my critique partners.
—A.H.

To my blondies Neva, Eloise and Greta.
To Amaya, real-life Ella, and all the
Solana Beach girls my sons grew up with.
—L.N.P.

Text copyright © 2020 by Amber Hendricks
Illustrations copyright © 2020 by Luciana Navarro Powell
Edited by Rebecca Glaser
Art direction and design by Christine Vanderbeek
Published in 2020 by Amicus Ink, an imprint of Amicus
P.O. Box 1329, Mankato, MN 56002
www.amicuspublishing.us

Library of Congress Cataloging-in-Publication Data
Names: Hendricks, Amber, author.
Powell, Luciana Navarro, illustrator.
Title: Extraordinary ordinary Ella / by Amber Hendricks;
illustrated by Luciana Navarro Powell.
Description: Mankato, MN : Amicus, [2020] | Summary: Ella is
not talented like her family and friends, but during the school
talent show she discovers just how extraordinary ordinary can
be when her acts of kindness steal the show.
Identifiers: LCCN 2019016553 (print) | LCCN 2019019240
(ebook) | ISBN 9781681525051 (ebook)
ISBN 9781681525020 (hardcover)
Subjects: | CYAC: Ability--Fiction. | Talent shows--Fiction.
Kindness--Fiction. | Individuality--Fiction.
Classification: LCC PZ7.1.H4633 (ebook) | LCC PZ7.1.H4633
Ext 2020 (print) | DDC [E]--dc23
LC record available at https://lccn.loc.gov/2019016553

First Edition 9 8 7 6 5 4 3 2 1

Printed in China

Ella was extraordinary.
Extraordinarily ordinary, that is.

Her sister, Carmen, floated
gracefully across the stage.

Ella tumbled over her toes.

Her cousin, Kenji, played
piano with precision.

Ella discovered a
new range of sound.

Her best friend, Maria,
whipped up decadent delights.

Ella whisked up a kitchen catastrophe.

It seemed like everyone at school had a talent. Everyone except Ella.

Her singing was shrill.

Her laps came in last.

Her poetry lacked pizzazz.

And Ella was a terrible speller—the WURST.

No matter how hard she tried, Ella was just Ella.
Extraordinarily, boringly, ordinary Ella.

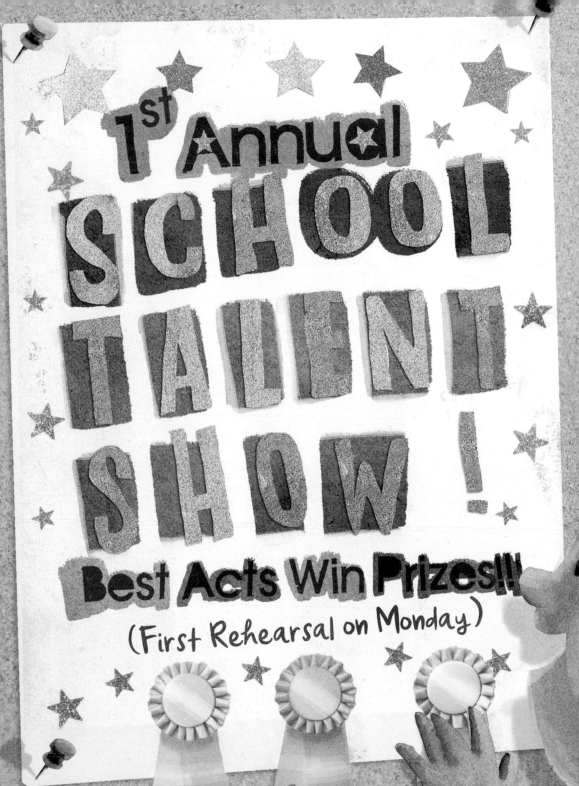

One day, Ms. Almazon made an announcement.

The school was hosting a talent show!

Ella traced the shiny ribbons.
This was her chance!

But she needed something BIG to prove that she was extraordinary too.

Tightrope walking?

Too scary.

Synchronized swimming?

Too wet.

Lion taming?

Ella wondered if she could borrow Mrs. Beasley's cat on such short notice.

On the first day of rehearsals,
Ella practiced pirouettes.

Her ribbon dipped and darted,
fluttered and twirled! Ella was feeling
pretty good about her routine until ...

But when Carmen's ballet slipper tore, Ella's ribbon was just the right fit.

The next day, Ella attempted juggling.

Her balls flipped and flew, circled and soared!

Ella was getting the hang of it until ...

Plonk!

Plonk!

Plonk!

But when Luke's dog Muffin played
tug-of-war with Cal's magic wand,
Ella's ball was a tempting trade.

Ella tried talent after talent after talent.

But nothing fit.

On the last day of rehearsals,
Ella still didn't have an act.

Kenji began practicing
Ella's favorite song and
she sang softly along.

But when Kenji was too nervous to remember the tune, Ella sang louder.

Muffin howled and her friends covered their ears. But Kenji giggled so hard he forgot all about his stage fright.

Finally, the day of
the big show arrived.

Everyone was ready.

Everyone except Ella.

She had been so busy helping her friends
that she still didn't have an act for the show.

Ella's friends took the stage.

Ella wished she were
a magician like Cal.

Or a dancer
like Carmen.

Or a musician like Kenji.

But without a talent, she
was still plain ordinary Ella.

Afterwards, when Ms. Almazon announced the winners,
the audience clapped wildly, and Ella cheered loudest of all.

But the show wasn't over yet.

"For extraordinary acts of kindness and a real talent for helping others,"
Ms. Almazon said, "our winners would like to say a special thank you to ..."

"...Ella!"

The audience burst into applause.
Ella couldn't believe her ears.

Kindness? Helping others?
That was just ordinary.
That was just Ella.

Maybe being ordinary wasn't so bad after all.
Extraordinarily ordinary, that is!